Scamper and the Airplane Thief

Danielle S. Marcotte
Illustrations by Paul Roux

Scamper and the Airplane Thief

1

Midtown Stories
Keep the Blue Side Up!

Scamper and the Airplane Thief
Copyright © Midtown Press, 2018.
All rights reserved.

ISBN 978-0-9881101-9-9
Legal deposit: Library and Archives Canada
Printed and bound in China

Editor: Louis Anctil
Assistant: Daniel Anctil
Illustrations, design and production: Paul Roux

Library and Archives Canada Cataloguing in Publication

Marcotte, Danielle S., 1952-
[Moustique et le voleur d'avion. English]
        Scamper and the airplane thief / Danielle Marcotte ; Paul Roux,
illustrator.

(Keep the blue side up! ; 1)
Previously published: 2014.
Previous edition illustrated by Francesca Da Sacco.
Translation of: Moustique et le voleur d'avion.
Previous title: Moosetick and the airplane thief.

        I. Roux, Paul, 1959-, illustrator II. Marcotte, Danielle S.,
1952- . Moosetick and the airplane thief. III. Title. IV. Title: Moustique
et le voleur d'avion. English V. Series: Marcotte, Danielle S., 1952- .
Keep the blue side up! ; 1

PS8626.A7364M6813 2018   jC813'.6   C2017-905540-2

To Bob, always the teacher.
To Annick, Claudio and Diego, uplifting friends.

"There's my friend, Spencer, flying with his bird family," says Scamper, the little red seaplane. He is watching the flock of Canada geese take off. "What a beautiful September day for a flight over the Fraser River! Will Teacher Bob bring a student for a lesson this morning?" he wonders. "And who will we coach next, a boy or a girl?" Scamper likes young people. After all, he is a Luscombe 8f, a training plane.

He looks towards the flight school.

He hopes to see his regular pilot, old Teacher Bob, when a young man comes out by the side door. He struts, all straight and overly confident, towards the seaplane. His baseball cap is turned backwards on his head. He wears ear buds. He carries keys and a steaming mug. "What is that student, Nate, doing alone on the

docks?" asks the seaplane.

"This young man is not experienced enough to pilot me on his own. I don't like the looks of this," worries Scamper. "It takes many lessons before a trainee can fly without his instructor. That is just the way it is done, for everyone's

safety. And Teacher Bob always sticks by the rules. I do, too. We try to prepare for any event, like engine problems, weather problems, **terrain** problems... I even made sure my friend Spencer knows to stay clear of my flight path so neither of us gets **hurt**. But I certainly never thought to plan for this, a **rogue** student!"

Bigger seaplanes at the dock gently poke fun at Scamper because he is so small and darts about like a little kid full of energy. That is how he got his nickname. The little plane doesn't mind. He senses it is done all in good fun. Scamper also knows he may be small, but his work with Bob is very important. And he definitely can tell right from wrong. "Hey, rookie," thinks the little seaplane, glaring at Nate, "Stay off my **pontoons**!"

But with a mischievous smile, Nate unlocks Scamper's door and puts down his hot drink and ear buds. "Little plane, you and I are going to show that old Teacher Bob a thing or two," he says. The young pilot unties the startled seaplane, forgets all the **safety checks**, and hops in the **cockpit**.

As Scamper's motor roars, Bob comes out of the office, clutching some papers in his hand. He runs onto the docks and yells: "Nate, stop! You have not written your **flight plan!**" But the young man and the worried seaplane are already in the middle of the river, picking up speed.

Nate looks back, amused at Teacher Bob waving at him on the dock. The old man usually moves slowly, his face crinkled into a smile under his old ball cap. This morning, he hops up and down by the water, like a mad frog. All sorts of maps and papers are flying everywhere. The old instructor tries to grab the young man's attention with his silly dance, despite the airplane's noise. He seems angry, but in fact, he is worried for his careless student.

The little seaplane is also very concerned for his pilot's safety. "Nate should be looking ahead, not backwards at Bob's reaction," frets Scamper "because we are too close to the power lines now for a safe takeoff." The plane makes his engine sputter to catch Nate's attention and it works.

Alerted by the strange noise, the

pilot finally turns around and looks ahead. He pulls back on the **stick** and the seaplane starts to **lift off**.

This is what Nate usually does when Bob coaches him. At this point in the training flight, the old instructor always says, "Easy does it!" with a lot of encouragement in his voice. But today Nate is alone in the cockpit. Something seems different. Is he missing the reassuring voice of the old man? "Certainly not!" thinks the student pilot. "This is fun! Finally, on my own!"

But, something nags at him, what is different today?

The young man suddenly realizes

he is much closer to the power lines than usual. "Oh my!" says Nate, as his heart starts to beat like crazy in his chest. "This does not look like it did the last time I took off, not at all!"

The big wires in front of him dip dangerously over the river. The seaplane is too low and too **slow** at this point to go over the power lines the usual way! The seaplane does not have enough speed for the pilot to pull way up over the cables. "Less speed means less power to control the plane," remembers Nate with a hint of panic.

"If I fly just slightly up and touch the wires, the plane could get tangled in them or worse, tumble, and fall down in the river. If we go too far down and hit the water at the wrong angle... well, we could also tumble upside down in the river! What a choice!" thinks Nate in the space of a few seconds.

"There is only one way, the middle path," realizes the pilot.

"We will have to go under the wires, between the cables and the water, not too high and not too low. Easy does it." His heartrate increases. Pressure builds up in his ears. His hands start shaking.

All of sudden, in his mind's eye, he sees his favourite superhero. This gives him courage. It helps him keep his thoughts organized and his hands steady. "I can do this," he mutters. "Little plane, stay with me, don't sputter out," says Nate through clenched teeth. It's as if he's the superhero and Scamper is his sidekick.

The seaplane responds well. He

does his best not to touch his reflection in the water and keeps a good distance from the wires.

Scamper has only one thought: he must save his pilot. The cables' shadows pass over his wings as they fly safely under the power lines. "We made it!" shouts the pilot with joy.

"What a relief!" sighs the seaplane. "Can we go home now, get Bob, and stop this silly business?"

"**Wow**, this is great!" says Nate. "I feel good. Let's go do some exploring."

"Oh no!" thinks Scamper. "We should really stick to our usual flight path, rather than go about like crazy grasshoppers. Better yet, we should return to the flight school. A lot could still go wrong."

The young man feels a great rush of excitement as he pulls Scamper's nose towards the sky. They fly up in the endless blue.

"I've wanted to do this for such a long time," says Nate. "How fun!"

With a big smile on his face, he then banks the plane to the left and to the right. The rolling motion also makes Scamper giddy with joy. He forgets his worries about the pilot's safety for a moment.

Both pilot and plane are now happy like little kids on a county fair ride. The pleasure of flying overpowers them and little else matters for a few

minutes. Filled with joy, they stop looking around them. "Nothing better than clear skies over me!" Nate sings to himself.

But what is this? A flock of Canada geese has suddenly appeared in front of the red plane and startled the young pilot. "Whoa, Nellie!" exclaims Nate, frozen in panic for a minute.

Scamper quickly comes out of his flying daydreams and emits a loud backfire... **"Bang!"**

This scares both the young man and the birds. In a tough spot, the pilot veers off one way and goes down to one side while the geese escape the other way.

Thanks to Scamper's quick reaction, they avoid hurting the geese with the propeller.

"That's not Nellie!" thinks Scamper. "It is my friend Spencer and his family. Good thing we did not hit them!"

The little plane is both happy to have saved the geese and mad at himself and Nate for their thoughtless flying.

But the sudden action to save the birds has sent Nate's hot drink all over the seaplane's **control panel**. Sparks are flying everywhere.

"**Argh**, I don't feel well at all," moans Scamper after a few minutes. His engine hiccups and shakes the pilot out of his seat.

"Oh, no!" cries out Nate with a hint of panic. The young man has never experienced this strange new sound and that weird shaking. How should he react? If only Bob were here to teach him what to do!

The plane continues to hiccup and to lose **altitude**. Below the wings, the many rivers and fields make a giant everchanging patchwork blanket. The pilot and plane are at once dazzled by it and a bit lost. They should have been more mindful and cautious. **Where are they?**

Scamper thinks, and he thinks some more, but no ideas come to him. "One thing is for sure, Nate should land as soon as possible. I see some water to the right. There is a quiet cove as well. We could go there and think over what to do, but he does not seem to be able to make a decision right now. What can I do to help him?"

While Scamper tries to find a quick solution, his anxiety builds up stress inside him. He does not realize it, but the tension works on his metal frame. To his surprise, his right wing emits a loud ping when the stress is suddenly released.

The noise startles the pilot. He turns his head to the right with a worried look. What is this new sound? For a few seconds Nate is surprised by the noise and also blinded by the glare of the sun shining on the water.

The sudden ping and the dazzling light are wake-up calls. They shake the student pilot out of his panic. "I should land the plane there, calm down, and inspect it for damage," realizes Nate. "But will I be able to?" he wonders.

The young man brings the seaplane down as quickly as he can. Luckily, a small breeze ripples the water slightly. These tiny waves make it easier for the nervous student to judge how to land. "I thank my lucky stars that this is not glassy water. It is so hard to get your bearings when the water is still!" sighs Nate. Through all this, Scamper feels ill but tries hard to reach the water safely. Sputtering, the seaplane is able to **touch down** all in one piece.

"This looks like a small river. Where are we exactly?" asks Nate while he lands safely on the water. "Oh! I forgot my maps!" he realizes, squinting into the sun, "and my sunglasses... come on little plane, let's make one last effort." The pilot can barely bring the pontoons' tips onto a sandbank in the middle of the river. Nate cuts the motor and jumps out onto the small sand island.

First, he checks his phone. "**Wow**, no reception," he realizes. "That's quite useless. And now, how will I get out of this mess?"

"I wonder if there is **tidal action** in this river. It could mean the sandbank is under water part of the day. I better find a solution soon."

As he surveys the area, something gives him hope. Forgetting all about Scamper, the pilot turns his back on the airplane, and runs across the sand island. On the other side of the water, there are people fishing far away on the river's edge. "Help!" screams Nate, jumping up and down on one side of the sandbank.

He does not notice the water's action behind him on the other side of the small island. While he is looking the other way, the waves are slowly moving Scamper back out onto the open water.

"Nate! Come back! I am not

anchored to anything and the current is taking me away!" rages the red plane. Too late! The water carries the little float plane more and more rapidly, away from the quiet cove nearby. "If only I could get to that cove, I would be safe," thinks Scamper "but how can I do that?" That is when he hears a friendly voice: "Need help, buddy?"

It is Spencer and his family of Canada geese flying in formation over him! "We thought you sounded distressed so we followed you."

"Spencer," says the little plane, thinking fast, "can you and your whole family stand on my right wing, please?" Gracefully, the geese circle over him and all land on his right wing.

The pontoon on the opposite side lifts off the water just enough for the plane to veer off the current and aim for the cove. "Thanks pal! It is great to have friends," sighs Scamper with relief.

Soon a girl and her father arrive at the cove. They were fishing nearby and they watched the whole adventure from the shore. Under their life jackets, they wear vests with many pockets to carry their fishing supplies. They tie the plane to a rock with seemingly endless lengths of fishing wire. Scamper is relieved and grateful. "Now," says the father, "let's go back and get help."

"But what about the pilot on the sandbank?" asks the girl.

"Oh, he is safe there until help arrives. I think he could use some thinking time," answers the father. Scamper could not agree more!

Teacher Bob

Glossary

Altitude: Height.

Cockpit: The front part of a plane where the pilot sits.

Control panel: The dials, also called instruments, and switches in front of the pilot's seat.

Flight plan: Information written by a pilot before he or she leaves with the plane. He or she writes the location the plane is leaving from, the destination it is going to, and the time of arrival. He or she also notes alternate airports that will be used in case of bad weather, and the number of passengers in the plane. If the plane is late, the rescuers then know where to search.

Hurt: Birds can represent a real danger for airplanes of all sizes, as they can dent them or get stuck in some moving parts, depending on the type of planes. Planes are also dangerous for birds as a collision can hurt or kill them.

Lift off: To lift off is when the plane rises in the air.

Pontoons: Watertight floats filled with air that seaplanes have instead of wheels.

Rogue: A person who does not follow the rules.

Safety checks: A pilot has a series of things to check before he or she takes off with an airplane, such as the level of fuel and oil.

Slow: An airplane must fly at a certain speed for the pilot to be able to control it and make it go up or sideways quickly. It is a bit like going up a hill on a bicycle. If you go too slowly, the bike stops and you may fall.

Stick: The pilot of the Luscombe 8f does not hold a wheel as if he or she were driving a car. The pilot's hands are on a stick that controls moving parts of the plane. This makes the plane go up and down and roll left and right.

Terrain: Ground. High mountain terrain can be a problem for a plane.

Tidal action: The sea goes up and down, once or twice a day. Rivers that are close to the sea can also go up and down. At certain times, parts of the river banks are under water. At other times, when water goes out, those same parts show sand banks and temporary islands.

Touch down: To touch down is when the plane makes contact with the ground, water or snow.